Yes, Marisol, There is a Santa Claus!

Jonathan McSurdy

Published by Red Moon Publishing
155 N. Main St.
Doylestown, PA 18901

Illustrations by Emery T. Perkins
Layout and Design by Angela Werner, Michael Höhne Design

1st Printing: June 2006

ISBN: 0-9785592-0-7

Marisol, remember the treasure

Jonathan P.
McSwnds

Thank You!

Emery Perkins

Marisol stretched out on her bed, staring glumly at the window where dainty white snowflakes danced across the pane. Outside she could hear her friends' happy shrieks as they ran around, playing in the light snow.

Normally, Marisol would be outside playing with Emma, Nick and Hannah, thrilled by the first snow of the season. It meant that winter was finally here, which meant that Christmas was almost here. And Christmas had always been Marisol's favorite holiday.

But not this year, she thought with a sigh.

"Marisol!" Tio Juan called suddenly from the living room. "Come!, It is time for us to go!"

Marisol didn't move. "Go where?" she called back.

"To the hospital," he replied.

The hospital?

Startled, she leapt off her bed and raced into the living room, where Tio sat talking with her mom.

"Are you sick, Tio? Is something wrong?"

"No, silly girl!" Tio teased her, grinning. "You and I are going to the hospital to visit some friends of mine. Come, it will be fun."

Fun? Marisol thought, reaching into the closet for her coat. A trip to the hospital to visit of bunch of old people certainly wasn't her idea of fun.

But she didn't say anything to Tio as she followed him out to his car. He was her favorite uncle—the one who always took her to the pool and read with her. No matter how glum she felt today, she didn't want to hurt his feelings.

As they drove downtown, they passed the huge Christmas tree that stood near City Hall. Tiny, multicolored lights dotted its branches. On top sat a huge gold star.

"The tree looks beautiful this year, doesn't it? Tio asked.

"I guess…" Marisol mumbled.

Tio cast her a surprised look. "Christmas is just two days away. You must be getting excited about Santa's coming."

She looked down at her boots. "Some of my friends are excited, but I'm not."

"You love Christmas, Marisol!" Tio exclaimed. "What's wrong?"

Marisol pulled off one of her mittens and fiddled with her seatbelt strap for a minute. "I'm almost ten, Tio," she said finally. "I'm not sure I believe in Santa Claus anymore."

"Ah…" Tio murmured, raising his eyebrows at her. "So that's it. Well, then," he went on, "I'll have to show you a different way of—"

Just then a child on a sled darted out in front of their car. Tio swerved, narrowly missing the child. Marisol was about to ask her uncle what he'd meant when they reached their destination: a tall glass building with a sign out front, Shriners Hospital.

They parked in a lot, and then entered the hospital through its wide glass doors. Tio pressed a button near the elevator, and moments later, they stepped out into a very large three story high play room.

"Hi Jon!" called someone.

Marisol looked up.

An adorable boy with blond hair sat in a wheelchair, both legs propped up in front of him. He was waving at Tio and grinning happily, showing two missing front teeth.

Tio grinned back at the boy. "Hi Matthew! How are you today?"

"Great," Matthew replied. He looked at Marisol. "What's your name?"

"This is my niece, Marisol," Tio said proudly. "She came with me to play some games today."

As they walked through the room, Tio introduced Marisol to many other children. A few were in wheelchairs like Matthew while others lay in beds, playing various games. Marisol noticed a common theme.

"Tio...What is this place?" she whispered. "All of the patients are children."

"It's a Shriners Hospital," he explained, "dedicated to helping children with injuries and disabilities.

"There are twenty-two of these hospitals," Tio went on. "Twenty are located in the U.S. and two others are in Mexico and Canada."

"But what is a...*Shriner?*" Marisol asked, carefully pronouncing the strange new word.

"A Shriner is someone like me who contributes time and money to help children get excellent medical care," Tio answered.

"Oh..." Suddenly Marisol understood. "So if it weren't for the Shriners...these kids might not have a chance to get better."

Tio nodded softly. "Shriners pay for all children's medical costs—and visit them in the hospital. We celebrate their birthdays, play with them….and help them learn to adjust and adapt to their world. Shriners have treated children from all over the world."

"Hi Tio!" a dark-haired girl called, coming toward them. Marisol saw that she had an unusual gait and walked with difficulty. "Want to play a game with me?"

"Sure, Emily," said Tio. "What'll be today—Life or Monopoly?"

"Life!" Emily answered. Moving very slowly, she made her way over to a tall shelf unit piled high with board games.

Tio introduced Marisol to Emily, who was also nine, Marisol learned. While they played Life, Emily chattered away, talking about her family and Christmas's coming soon and her favorite sport, soccer.

"How did you get hurt?" Marisol asked a short while later, hoping Emily didn't mind her asking the question.

"I was riding my bike and got hit by a car," Emily replied matter-of-factly. "I injured my spinal cord."

"Oh...." Marisol said sympathetically. "That sounds hard."

"It is," Emily agreed with a nod. "But I'm very lucky to be at Shriners Hospital."

After they'd finished playing Life, the three of them played a round of Monopoly. When that game finally ended, Tio glanced at his watch. "It's time for us to go," he told Marisol.

"Thanks for playing with me," Emily said. Then she shot Tio a sly look. "It was fun to beat you—again!"

Tio grinned. "It's always my pleasure to lose to you!"

Emily turned to Marisol. "It was nice to meet you."

"You, too," Marisol answered. She really liked this friendly, spirited girl.

"I hope you'll come back," Emily told her.

"She'll be back," Tio promised. "I'll bring her again after Christmas."

Marisol looked away for a minute, feeling bad at the mention of the holiday. What kind of Christmas would Emily have? she wondered. It couldn't be much fun when you were stuck in a hospital.

But to her surprise, the other girl's face brightened.

Almost reading Marisol's thoughts, Emily exclaimed "Oh, I'll have a great Christmas this year, Santa Claus has already come, giving me the most wonderful gifts!"

Marisol and Tio said good-bye and left, with Marisol deep in thought.

As they walked back to the parking lot, Marisol was filled with questions.

"Why did Emily seem so *happy* about Christmas, Tio? What did she mean, Santa has already come?"

"Emily has had many operations since her accident," Tio explained. "The doctors said she would never walk again. But since her last surgery, she has spent many, many hours in physical therapy. And just a few weeks ago, she took her first steps in more than three years!"

"Whoa…" Marisol breathed. "That's amazing."

Tio nodded. "It certainly is. Soon she will be wearing braces on her legs and walking even greater distances. And who knows? Perhaps one day she'll be able to run and kick a soccer ball again."

Marisol was lost in her thoughts as they drove back home through the snowy city streets.

The doctors had told Emily she'd never walk again? And she'd been in and out of the hospital for a whole three years? Meanwhile Marisol had been going to school everyday and running around and riding her bike....

"That's why Emily told me that Santa has already visited her!" she blurted out. "Because she's finally able to walk again!"

"Yes, Marisol," Tio answered softly. "That's right."

Marisol looked at her uncle, wondering about something. "Why do you volunteer at the Shriners Hospital, Tio?"

"Long ago, when I was a child, I was a patient at a Shriners Hospital, too," he explained. "It's my way of giving back. To say thank you for the gift I once received. And it is the unconditional nature of the gift which is in the very spirit of Christmas."

"I think the Shriners are a lot like Santa," Marisol said thoughtfully. "But they bring gifts to children all year round."

Tio flashed her a bright smile and simply nodded. "Shriners give children hope. Hope is the best of things, sometimes it's all these kids wish for."

Marisol leaned her head against the car window, watching the snowflakes drift down from the sky. Under the streetlamps' glow, they sparkled like tiny diamonds.

How beautiful, she thought. Happiness suddenly spread through her. Christmas was coming soon, and now she knew just what to believe—there really was a Santa Claus, who delivered miracles everyday.

Helping Miracles Happen...

Tina

Saksen

DALTON

Courtney

Mark

Ethel P

MIRANDA

Breyana

Jamir

Jose

Thank You!

For more information regarding the Shriners philanthropy,
please visit their website at
www.shrinershq.org

If you know of a child that Shriners Hospital may help:
1.800.237.5055

For more information on the Shriners international fraternity:
1.800.537.4746

MALI *Marisa♡

JRN

Annette

About the Author

Jonathan P. McSurdy was born, raised and currently lives in Bucks County, Pennsylvania. He was a former patient of Shriners Hospitals, and has become a Shriner. He is part of the international public relations campaign for the Shriners Hospital System. Jonathan speaks at various local engagements promoting the charity, and he does ride horses in Shriners parades. All proceeds of this book will benefit charity.

About the Artist

Emery T. Perkins was born in upstate New York, and moved to Pennsylvania with his family at the tender age of ten. Jonathan and Emery became acquainted while working together. Emery's passions include motorcycling and travel. He has traveled most of the United States, Canada and Mexico on a motorcycle. Now he and his fiancée share in their traveling passions. Emery has an artist's sensibility, and an artist's sense of humor. Emery sincerely hopes you have enjoyed the illustrations in this book, and thanks you for the donation you have made to charity by purchasing this tome.

About Marisol

Marisol Reina Gilbert is 11 years old and is in fifth grade. She lives in Ottsville, Bucks County with her mom and her dogs Darby & Tucker. She plays on the soccer, basketball, and track teams at her school. Marisol loves spending time with her Uncle Jonathan, who has given her many gifts, including the love of reading and memorable visits with the children at Shriners Hospital.